Gwermie the Gwermkin

Lael

Believe in yourself and you can do anything.

C Fiske

by Christopher Fiske
illustrated by Chen Ly

Gwermie the Gwermkin

by Christopher Fiske
illustrated by Chen Ly

One day
I was laying on the cool green grass in the garden
watching the clouds float by
imagining them to be amazing shapes
There I fell asleep.

Some time must have passed
for now the sun was beginning to go down.
As I opened my eyes there laying next to me
was the most peculiar creature.
I have never seen you in the garden before.
What are you?

After he blinked, yawned, and stretched
He said to me

My mom tells me
I am a one of a kind
never to be created again
always under foot

Gwermie the Gwermkin.

I laughed.

What is a Gwermkin?

I am a Gwermkin he said.

I live in the garden. I like to eat new potatoes, tender carrots, and sweet peas. But most, most, most of all I like to

SNUGGLE

And with that he jumped into my arms
burrowed his furry head under my chin
and fell fast asleep.

I laid him under the lettuce
Went inside the house
And wondered if I would ever see

the Gwermkin again.

One winter night
when the snow had covered the
garden I woke to find the

Gwermkin

It is so very cold out he said.
Can I please snuggle with you
until the sun comes up?
Of course, you are always
welcome here.
He smiled.

And with that he jumped into my arms
burrowed his furry head under my chin
and fell fast asleep.

When I got sick the next
summer and had to stay inside.
I was laying there wishing I was
out playing.
I looked over and saw the

Gwermkin.

You don't look very well he
said.
I don't feel very well and I have
to stay inside to get better.

He smiled.

And with that he jumped into my arms
burrowed his furry head under my chin
and fell fast asleep.

While trying to help in the kitchen
I accidentally made a big mess
and was sent to my room.
I stomped off and sat there in a
grumpy mood. Looking over I

saw the Gwermkin.

Why are you grumpy he said?
I don't know.
I don't want to talk about it.

He smiled.

And with that he jumped into my arms
burrowed his furry head under my chin
and fell fast asleep.

One evening when it was time for me to go to bed
As I started to fall asleep I heard my mom whisper to me
You are my one of a kind
never to be created again
always under foot

Gwermie the Gwermkin.

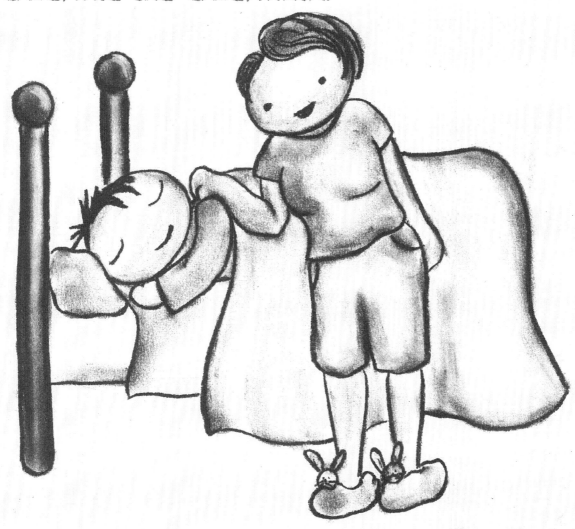

The End.

Special Thanks to:
God, Douglas, Missy, Buster, Mom, Dad, and Chen

Gwermie the Gwermkin

encourages children to be creative so he
has added blank 'imagination pages' to
draw, color, and write a story.

Imagination Page

Imagination Page

Imagination Page

Imagination Page

Imagination Page

Imagination Page

Imagination Page

Imagination Page

Imagination Page

Imagination Page

Imagination Page

Imagination Page

Made in the USA
Lexington, KY
25 September 2011